Clint Faraday
#19
A Moving Target

Light planes are being shot down over the comarca. Clint is called because he can get information others can't. What's behind it? What do the Indios have that can shoot down a plane three kilometers away? What is it about?

Clint Faraday
#19
A Moving Target
© 2011 & 2018 by C. D. Moulton

This is a work of fiction. Any resemblances to persons, living or dead, or events is purely coincidental unless otherwise stated.

Clint Faraday
#19
A Moving Target

Contents

About the author

CD was born in Lakeland, Florida. His education is in genetics and botany. He has traveled over much of the world, particularly when he was in music as a rock rhythm guitarist with some well-known bands in the late sixties and early seventies. He has worked as a high steel worker and as a longshoreman, clerk, orchidist, bar owner, salvage yard manager and landscaper – among other things.

CD began writing fiction in 1984 and has more than 115 books published as of this time in SciFi, murder, orchid culture and various other fields.

He now resides in Bocas del Toro and David, Panamá, where he continues research into epiphytic plants. He loves the culture of the indigenous people and counts a majority of his closer friends among that group. Several have "adopted" him as their father. He funds those he can afford through the universities where they have all excelled. "The Indios are very intelligent people, they are simply too poor (in material things and money. Culturally, they are very wealthy) to pursue higher education."

CD loves Panamá and the people. He plans to spend the rest of his life in the paradise that is Panamá

- Estrelita Suarez V.

CD is involved in research of natural cancer cure at this time. It has proven effective in all cases, so far. It is based on a plant that has been in use for thousands of years, is safe, available, and cheap. He has studied botany, and was cured of a serious lymphoma with use of the plant, *Ambrosia peruviana*.

Information about this cure is free on the FaceBook page, Ambrosia peruviana for cancer. CD asks only that all who try it please report on its effectiveness on that group.

A Moving Target

<u>A Call</u>

Clint Faraday, retired PI from Florida, USA, tied his boat to the deck of his Isla Colón home and helped his attractive next door neighbor, Judi Lum, step onto the deck. They just arrived back from a visit to Cusapín, a paradise puebla on a peninsula into the Caribbean to the southeast of Isla Colón. They unloaded the gifts and special foods, then their gear. Judi said she needed a long cool shower, then was going to loaf around for the rest of the day. Clint said that sounded like a plan to him!

He cleaned the boat, then went in to take the cool shower he'd promised himself. That done, he checked his new e-mail to find fifty some-odd advertisements he deleted and four messages he answered. He then got a cold Balboa from the 'fridge and laid in his hammock to enjoy it.

The phone rang. He ignored it.

His cellular buzzed. He sighed and looked at the caller ID. Capt. Genio Morales, Panamá City, Policía Nacional?

"Yo, Genius! Como esta?"

"Bien, gracias, Clint. I have a bit of a problem here that you might be able to help with.

"A light plane landed at Albrook yesterday with four bullet holes in it. About an hour ago a plane was shot down – the pilot radioed that he was under fire – in Darien.

"It's been awhile since we had anything like this. The only thing we can connect is that they were both blue and white, and both were pontoon planes. It's not a terrorist thing. We don't have that here. I want to request, officially, that you aid us in this. Most of the people there are Indigenos. They won't talk with the police since the trouble about their land. They'll talk to you."

Clint thought a minute, then said he'd call back in about an hour. He rang off and called Manolo, an undercover agent for Interpol et al. He said it wasn't anything to do with drugs or art theft that he'd received any information about.

Clint thanked him, sat back to think, then called Genio to say he'd be in Panamá City early in the morning.

It was a bit drizzly when he landed at Albrook, in Panamá City, but would clear up soon. This time of the year had some rain, but the really wet season was a month away. Genio was waiting to take him to a briefing at the station. He was filled in on what they knew, to this point, which wasn't much more than he'd reported on the phone. Clint would be given transportation anywhere he wanted to go. At the briefing, he was told that there were some suggestions that it was about a big European company wanting to dispossess the Indios from a part of the comarca in Darien. The present rumor was that there were some corrupt politicians – something that Panamá has more than its share of – wanting to grab the land on a ruse, but no one knew what was behind it. Other than the fact it was beautiful land, which is also something Panamá has in vast quantity, no one knew what was found there. Those were no developers, they were a company or two.

"So. Why call me? – the truth. I don't play games."

"You can get those people to talk. We can't," Genio explained. "The Indios, if they know, will tell you anything you want to know. After all, you *are* declared a Ngobe!"

Clint had the great honor of two chiefs in the comarcas in Bocas del Toro declaring him a Ngobe. By law, he was now a native Panamanian Indio.

"You don't have a clue? Can't you trace who owns those planes and find out?"

"No. The first one is privately owned by a man in the timber business, from Brasil. The second one was a tourist from France who isn't associated with any company. The

Brasilian has no business interest here, other than using the canal – which isn't something he's directly involved in."

"Then I just don't get it. Is someone shooting down any blue and white light plane that flies over?"

"That's more or less what we're afraid of. Someone who shoots down any light plane until he gets the one he wants. There are enough nuts here without something like this."

"All I can do is try, which I will. You can take me to the place they were shot at. We'll have that much!"

"Except they were a hundred four kilometers apart, give or take ten."

"Crap!"

"Uh-huh. I won't blame you if you tell us to stick it."

"Not my nature! I'm curious. I like the Indios. It's a place I know very little about. I'll go."

The chopper dropped Clint and his baggage off in a little village called Las Piedras. It was named after several large boulders, almost stone hills, near a small river. It was lush rain forests, at that altitude. He could expect a lot of rain.

One of his favorite gripes was tourists who came to a tropical rain forest and complained because it rained so much. People can be unbelievably stupid. He was apt to tell them they could go back to wherever they came from and it wouldn't be a problem.

He was greeted a bit formally. No one here knew him, so he spoke in Ngobere. It wasn't the same dialect as these, but some of them knew the language. He said his name was Clint Faraday, and that he was Ngobe. A woman said she had heard of him. He would be welcomed here – and did he know a man called Obilio Acosta?

"Jon. (Yes. Pronounced 'Hone')"

"He is a cousin on my mother's side. He is second chief in a place in the comarca."

"Yes, I know. Cusapín. I know him and Silvio very well. Silvio is one who declared me Ngobe. Cusapín is paradise."

"Much of Panamá is paradise. I am Nilsa. This is Armando, this is Elena, and this is my man, William. You wish to stay here?"

"I don't know yet. I'm trying to find some information about the planes being shot down, and that may be elsewhere."

She nodded. "That information is known only by rumor, and is here as much as anywhere else in the comarca. You are welcome in my house."

Clint thanked her and took his pack to the house, which looked like a hut, from outside, but was comfortable and clean inside. They had running water because they piped it from the mountain with PVC pipe. People were often surprised to find the Indios had running water in their houses. They had it before the white man came. Where the PVC was laid now had once had bamboo split down the middle and made into a trough that delivered the waters, though now it was in all the houses by direct pipeline, while before they carried it in buckets from a central container.

Clint was full of such facts, and was constantly impressed by the practical intelligence of the people.

Clint then went with Armando to walk around the pleasant village, meeting everyone. Several knew about him from friends when they went into the cities to sell vegetables and products from the comarca. They chatted about anything that came up, mostly about friends and distant family members in other places that Clint had visited. He got a little information, mostly, as Nilsa said, rumor. He did learn that two city-type men came several times, but they didn't have much to discuss here. That meant it was somewhere else. Clint learned that most of the talk about those idiots trying to steal the land was from a village to the east.

Clint stayed there for two nights, then called Genio to have the chopper take him farther east. He didn't know anything more than that it was located east of the village where he was staying. It wasn't close, or these people would know more.

He went on, having made twenty six more friends.

About sixty kilometers farther east they came to another village about the same size as Las Piedras. This one was called Green Water (in translation). There was a small lake with alga that made the water green. It was almost a kilometer away, and the people didn't go there. It was simply a landmark. Still water was usually full of parasites, so they would avoid it.

They were met with open suspicion by some. That told Clint he was close to where he would find information. These were not a suspicious people, generally. If there was any small suspicion of strangers, it would be with damned good reason.

Clint mentioned Nilsa and William. Most knew them, knew of them and their village. If Clint came because they sent him, they knew he was a good man.

Clint said, "They did not send me. They only said that the information I seek is to the east. This is to the east of Las Piedras." He wouldn't lie to these people. Ever. Not even by omission.

"You know them well?" Generoso, an old man, asked.

"I stayed in their home the past two nights."

"Then it is the same.

"Do you know a man called Silvio?"

"Several. Cusapín?"

"Yes."

"He declared me Ngobe, much to my pride."

He nodded. "Then you will stay with me. I have room. Come."

Clint took his pack from the chopper, it left as he went with Roso to a comfortable house, much like William's. He had Genio send some things on the chopper he presented to Roso. Practical things for the house. Knives, spoons, coffee mugs, and some stainless steel pans – and one silly gift for friendship. A Panamá hat. It would be placed on a peg on the wall. If Roso ever went to another village or a city, he would wear it. There was absolutely no other use for such a thing.

That is a strange custom among several groups of Indios. Roso was delighted with the gift for the idea it conveyed. Clint was totally accepted. If he didn't fully accept Roso as a friend, he wouldn't have presented the hat, just the useful objects.

They spent the rest of the day with Clint getting acquainted with the people. There were forty three people, he met them all. He told them, frankly, why he was there. They would meet tomorrow with the ones who knew anything to discuss what Clint would do with any information they gave. Clint understood that the law of the cities and most of Panamá was not the law on the comarca. They would want to be sure no officials from outside would come there to cause trouble. That was less than no problem at all with Clint Faraday. He was among the first who didn't want intrusion by government on the comarcas.

Ronaldo, a young man, came to Roso's with several others. He had a guitar that looked familiar. Clint asked about it.

"I was north, at Las Cañas. There was a gringo there to study plants. He had it, and learned that I played some, so I played some songs. He was once a rock guitarist. He said I have the touch. I must practice a lot to be so good. I told him I couldn't practice much because four of us had one guitar to use. He gave it to me.

"He is a crazy gringo, but crazy in a good way."

"Dave?"

"Yes! You know him?"

"He is a close friend. He lives in Bocas some, and in David some. He goes all over the country, studying orchids."

"He said he has a friend who would help us if we ever needed help. You are that friend, Clint Faraday?"

"Yes. I am here because I heard there was trouble from some gringos that was to the point the people were shooting down the planes of a certain type. You have shot two that are not involved in any way. I want to find who you seek. I'll put a stop to them."

"We will talk tomorrow. Tonight we sing and tell macho lies."

"Yes. Like the six young women who drive me crazy with their demands of constant sex. It can be a great burden to be so sexy to women."

These kinds of things were stories for fun. Everyone knew they were just that, and tried to make a better one. Clint had given them a hard one to top!

It was a great night. They didn't use alcohol, but they did have a plot where they grew some good pot. It was used only on special occasions and for medicine, particularly for eye problems. The Indios have used it for many centuries for medicine. They used it for relaxation and recreation very rarely. That they brought it out for Clint was another example of how he was accepted and liked by the people here. He liked them, too.

Tomorrow was soon enough to start his investigation. He would have full cooperation. He had trust – both ways, for and from.

It rained in the early morning hours and was still drizzling at five thirty when he awoke and went outside to the fire, where Roso had fresh coffee (Really fresh! He had dried and mashed it only the day before!) brewing. He, like Silvio in Cusapin, put in a few cacao beans when he mashed the coffee beans. It gave the coffee a very pleasant taste.

They went to the river to bathe, and caught a nice large fish of a type Clint didn't know. It would be their lunch. Roso had a girlfriend who would cook it for them. She could use the large pot Clint brought.

The Indios have no ownership of useful items. Roso would own the hat, but not the silverware or pans and such. Everyone would use those things, though they would stay mostly in his house. When anyone needed a large pot, they would go to his house. If it wasn't in use, they would take it. Everyone would know they had it for when it was needed by anyone else.

They would discuss the interloper problem after lunch. Clint would spend the morning helping Roso or anyone else who could use a hand in something. He mostly helped harvest yuca and plantains. Roso had a large plot of beets and potatoes. He had onions and garlic and a few other common root crops. The next plot had several varieties of peppers, picante and sweet, and tomatoes of three types. Next was beans of several varieties. There was a plot of sugar cane near the river. The soil was rich here, the main reason the village was here. What they didn't use in the village was traded to others or sent once a week to a (relatively) nearby town for sale. They used the money to buy rice, salt, and a few other items, such as laundry soap and brushes – and machetes. Those were the basic tool used on the comarcas. The jungle encroached in almost no time, meaning it required constant trimming. Monkeys came to watch, and parrots of three types were noisy neighbors.

Clint loved this place. It was paradise on a par with Cusapín!

They went in for lunch around noon. Nita, Roso's twenty-something girlfriend, had made a delicious meal of rice and red beans with fried fish and a soup with yucca, potatoes, onion, green peppers, white beans, and fish. This was a typical meal. Often, the meat would be chicken or iguana. Pork or beef was only when they came from a town, and only that day. Their cows and pigs were sent to market when they had too many. The cows were milked and the milk used the day it was taken. They made some cheese, but not much. Without refrigeration, it would spoil too quickly.

Everything was here for a very easy and pleasant life. The Indios didn't need to ask when there was any work to be done. It is part of the culture that everyone did their part. Even the children had work to do when they were seven or eight years old. It was an expected thing, and was not questioned. They share almost everything on the comarcas – and that included work.

Clint remembered when JFK said, "Ask not what your country can do for you, but what you can do for your country." That was the "always" philosophy of the Indigenos on the comarcas. Substitute "puebla" for "country" and you had the philosophy down pat. The

Indios didn't have the greeds of the "civilized" world to contend with.

Clint loved this place and these people. He could happily live here for the rest of his life – which was a lie. He would revert back to wanting things, and knew it. He could be happy for a few months, or even a year, but it would go sour. He knew it. That caused an emotional ache inside him.

Philosophical time's over! Time to meet and discuss what was going wrong for the people here. He definitely would do everything in his power to stop it.

"You know of the trouble with the copper," Eladio said. "We had much trouble because they wanted to open-pit mine on our land. We would not and we will not permit it. We know of the methods to get the attention of other countries. They would have to come and kill many of us to have that kind of mine here. The world would refuse them business.

"We know the copper is important to Panamá, and we know it must be mined. We only want it done in a way where the whole area will not become a wasted poisonous sore on the earth.

"We think probably it is the same people from another place who discovered the copper. They have found something here. They have no conscience, except for money. They will not aid Panamá, only themselves. They have now come here to demand things from us and to threaten us.

"That is what the government does not tell you. You do not know, or you would not be here unless to help us.

"They cannot intimidate us with their guns and armies.

Their armies cannot do anything in this kind of place, and we can have guns. They think they can come in the avions and shoot people and we cannot stop them.

"We can shoot, too. We told them to go and to not again come onto the comarca. They came in an avion and shot two people. We told them we would kill ten of them for every one of us they killed. We will not allow their avions over the comarca.

"You said the two of them who were shot are not involved. That is perhaps true of the one that did not fall. It is not true of the other, which did fall."

"This is determined to be fact?" Clint asked.

"Yes. The one was the pilot, and the other was one who shot Juan and Beto. He was shooting at us when we shot him down. He was not killed when the avion fell. Only the pilot. He was dead two minutes after it fell. There are eighteen to go before it is again even."

"Is the only way to tell which are theirs are the blue and white avions?"

"Blue and white with the floaters beneath and the symbol on the tail," Roso said.

"I was told of no symbol."

"No. The government does not want anyone to know. It would show they knew who those people are and what they are doing."

"What is the symbol?"

Eladio was handed a cell phone with a camera. Clint was shown the wreckage of the plane they shot down. It wasn't in bad shape, but the cockpit was pierced with a large limb that the pilot was impaled on.

"It would appear that the modern cellulars with the cameras do have some use," Eladio confided.

The symbol was clear on the last picture. It was a yellow flower with a lightning bolt going through it. It would be small, about ten inches in diameter. There were letters just under the symbol, but Clint couldn't read them. He said he wished he had some way to charge the batteries in his computer, so he could download and blow them up.

"We can charge the batteries. We have the solar panel to charge the cellulars," Roso said. "It is slow, but you will not need a very large charge to download the pictures."

Clint agreed. He also would charge his own cellular. Genio would have to come up with an explanation as to why he didn't tell Clint about several things. The way he'd acted, he probably didn't know. If some bigshit with the government wanted to cover up things, it would be easy to do so. He also wanted to know what they found here.

He chatted awhile, but wouldn't make any suggestions until he knew what it was about and what they were up against. It could get very dangerous if some of those old crooked powerful politicians were involved. If they controlled the information the police received, it would be a non-investigation. Clint remembered the trouble over the land theft from Dave. It drug on and on. The lawyer he had originally was actually being paid by the ones who falsified the papers to drag it out until it was turned over to the, in effect, dead file department. When he learned of that, he got another lawyer who went to the fiscalia to learn that they had also apparently bribed the judge to close the investigation.

Clint suddenly had another question he wanted answered.

"What kind of gun do you have that can shoot that effectively from that distance?"

It was a question that was definitely not going to be

answered, not because they didn't trust Clint, but because they had sworn to never give the information to anyone. That meant they would never give the information to anyone.

Four hours later the computer had enough of a charge to download the camera, and his cell phone had enough charge to use – but there was no signal there. He blew up the symbol to read the letters, GHKBHSA. It was a corporate plane. He was sorry he didn't have Genio take him to see the plane with the bullet holes in it. If that one had the symbol, someone owed him a few very damned pertinent explanations.

"Roso, did you see any of those people here? Did they say what they wanted, in any way?"

"They came, two of them, once, and three, once, to say they were going to bring in some heavy tractors and so forth here to our village because there was noplace closer to where they were going to work to bring it in, and they couldn't land those heavy avions on the lake. They did not ask could they bring it. They said they were bringing it.

"Paulo told them they had no permission to bring anything onto the comarca, and certainly had no permission to work, even with a machete.

"The fat one – Victor, they called him – said they could go anywhere they liked anytime they liked for whatever reason they liked on national land. I said this is not national land, it is the comarca.

"He was a fat, obnoxious, self-important ass! He said they had already spent more than five million dollars studying their project and weren't about to let us cheat them for more money.

"Rudolfo said we have no use for their money. They

would not come here for any reason.

"The one they called Allen said anyone who tried to stop them would die and rot on the spot.

"I said for every person they hurt here, ten of them would be hurt to the same degree. If they killed anyone, ten of them would die. We all told them to leave, and to not come back.

"The one they called Victor said to show us who is the chief here, and the one they called Blackie – he was mostly the flyer of the avion – pulled a pistol from his pocket, but Naldo was right there and took it away from him We then drove them to their avion on the lake with the bamboo whips. The fat pig squealed like a pig! I thought his heart would stop before we got there. He was red in the face, and couldn't breathe, but they got there. We didn't hit them, except at first, when they refused to go. They left.

"The next day the avion was back, low over the trees. Enrique and Somos were shot.

"We called a friend who had said he would make something when they were going to mine the copper lode that would make it impossible for them to use any equipment. It would make holes in even the biggest. He gave a messenger the thing and told him how to use it. It is not large and ... is very certain.

"We find it really will make holes in things. It makes holes in the avions from three kilometers away!

"We do not want this. If the government tries to come onto the comarca, we will use it then, too. If they make those ladrones stay away, there will be no more problems."

Clint nodded. He went to the top of the nearby mountain later and called Genio to tell him to send the chopper. There were some very serious questions that had to be answered before he could decide what to do – which damned well could be to help these people shoot down any planes that flew over the comarca at less than ten thousand feet.

The rest of the day and night were spent in getting to know the people. They were as simple, pragmatic, and fatalistic as most of the Indios. They were very intelligent, and wanted nothing more than to be left alone to live their lives with dignity.

Clint meant to see they were left alone and that they could live their lives with dignity.

<u>*How?*</u>

The chopper came about an hour after dawn. Genio was in it, so Clint introduced him to his new friends. He told them he would try to have the planes stopped, and would try to find who was doing this, and what they had found.

"I will come back here soon. Try to find exactly where they plan to do anything. See if they left anyone there."

"Genio will help with this? It is certain?"

Genio looked shocked when Clint replied, "I will have to see. It will depend on the complete honesty on all of our parts. If there is evasion or lying, that person or those people are enemies. Because of what has already happened, I will have to know more before I can honestly say this or that one is a friend."

Genio was very quiet as they got on the chopper to head back. He finally said, "Clint, you are a friend. What is wrong?"

"Did you see that plane that had the bullet holes in it?"

"Only from a long distance. I did not examine it, personally."

"How did you determine that the pilot wasn't involved? That he was from France? The first was from Brasil?"

"It was in the papers presented. The one from France, Duquesne, was with a passport from Argentina. He has a residency there for six months of the year. The Brasilian, Madeira, is from Brasil."

"The registry of the planes supported that?"

"The planes? The one from Argentina was the only one I read the papers of. It was a private small plane from Argentina that was leased by Duquesne. He was the owner and leased it to himself so he could use it as a legal business deduction. He told me that, because we have nothing to say about taxes in Argentina here."

"It didn't seem strange that he was using a business plane here in Panamá when he wasn't here on business? Just a tourist?"

"I never thought about it, to be quite honest. I agree, now, that it should have caught my attention."

"Is the plane still here?"

"Yes. It is being repaired. Duquesne is staying at the Hotel Europa."

"I have to see that plane. I believe you're telling the truth, so someone's lying their ass off to you. Those people killed two Indios. I have to know what it's about. I have to know who Blackie, Victor, and Allen are."

"Possibly Victor Karnovich? The Ruso who sometimes is with Duquesne?"

"A fat obnoxious asshole pig?"

"To be kind to him, but to insult pigs."

"He's the one who ordered that the Indios be killed. I think I want to know everything there is to know about that one."

"He is supposed to be Ruso mafia. We don't have anything we can charge him with."

"You will. Soon!"

They flew into Albrook and went to the hangar where the plane was being repaired. The man working on it said the shots were certainly high-powered! They went through the wing, through steel braces and out through the top without even expanding! That meant very high-point titanium-steel slugs, and a tremendous muzzle velocity.

"Not expanding?" Clint asked.

"Yeah. The hole was smooth and exactly the same diameter the last place it hit as the first. A softer slug, or one moving at a lower velocity, will mushroom or fragment as it penetrates. This one didn't. It's like it was done with a laser beam, you know? I know none of them would be that effective at more than a couple of feet."

"I don't know of any such thing, either," Clint replied. "I begin to be suspicious of something ... two things I was told. It would fit with something else someone once told me. It would pretty well fit the personality, too. Thanks for the information!"

They were walking away when Clint shook his head and said, "We might be in one hell of a fix! I hope it stays where it is, which can't happen if we don't stop it now."

"Tell me what must be done to stop it now, and it will be done! Immediately!" Genio cried. "There is a company logo on the tail! This is not a private aircraft!"

"See that no plane flies lower than ten thousand feet over that comarca. See that no one who even might maybe just possibly be tied into that company or any that does business with it goes onto the comarca for any reason."

"I can do some of that. Is it because someone is taking some new science fiction weapon onto the comarca? I do not like your reaction, even a little. You seem actually frightened – and Clint Faraday fears nothing nor no one!"

"The weapon's there already. I don't want anything to happen that could get it out of the Indios' hands. I don't want anyone to even suspect it exists. Believe me, I can't picture how ... I'm just connecting things I've heard, and the people I've heard them from and about ... it would fit the personality. Christ almighty, this is one hell of a scary thing, no matter how you look at it!

"Why in fucking hell does this kind of thing happen in Panamá, among the Indios? Why isn't it in Germany or Russia or somewhere you'd expect to find ... Christ!"

"Well, you do have Victor. He's Ruso, but I think not the science type. Maybe a business mogul who is used to people moving as he says, when he says, as far as he says, in the direction he says. He doesn't ask, he tells. They say KGB. I tend to believe that."

"That seems to be what everyone sees in him. We'll have to get him used to taking orders, not giving them. Where does he live?"

"On one of the private islands, but he stays at the Europa when he's ... as does Duquesne. So!"

Clint nodded. "So, indeed."

Clint went to the Hotel California to use his laptop. He had good reception for the internet, so checked first on GHKBHSA.

It seemed it was an "affiliate" of HKBHSA. Hong Kong Best Habitats Shanghai Associates. The "G" was Georgia. The US?

He checked the location of the main office. Georgia, alright! Not the US state. The old USSR state. That would explain Victor. "Habitats" would indicate they were basically land developers. The company was supposed to be an engineering consultant and mapping company.

Mapping? Engineering? "Habitats" was generally spoken of as housing, but the word had a lot of meanings. It could be the place anything was found, though usually among living things. "Natural habitat" was used in all botanical and zoological studies.

This didn't make a whole lot of sense. They wanted to bring in heavy equipment, so what they'd found wasn't any plant or animal that was only found in that area.

The area wasn't too far from the copper mines. Cinnabar was found in Panamá, but not in that kind of place. Gold and silver weren't known to be in that area. Zinc and such weren't. Platinum definitely wasn't. Radioactives weren't.

What could it be? There was sulfur in that kind of place, but the demand wasn't enough for anyone to try to mine it in the area. What was in demand that would make it worth the trouble and expense? He checked the computer sites for each valuable element, in a decreasing value order. Things like sand could be valuable in large pure mines in some places, but that wasn't under consideration here.

Potassium. Plentiful. Phosphorus was in locations that might make it a possibility, but was there that much market for it?

He checked the world supply. A lot came from Florida, as he knew. The mines around Lakeland were ... running out? There was too much opposition to expanding the mines into the less productive areas, because of the environmental damage they brought with them. Radium was found in phosphorus deposits?

Pretty even distribution. Barely worth cost of extracting. Not much demand for it.

He looked up the prices and quantities. The uses of phosphorus were well-known. Detergents didn't use them anymore. Fertilizers were the main use. Certain explosives. The list of uses was pages, but none of it seemed to be the kind of thing that would make it take on a higher value.

He was on page four of uses when he stopped. He went back to the first page to note the tonnages needed for the fertilizer trade today. Impressive. He took each item, and added the tonnages. It was getting to a figure far above what Clint would have ever considered.

There was a short piece with a link to a page printed many years ago in a SF magazine. Isaac Asimov. He noted that the most limited supply of an element critical to continuing life on Earth was phosphorus. The main supplies for the Americas were ... Florida. Other deposits weren't nearly so productive.

Florida was running out. European, Chinese, and African lodes weren't as pure or as large.

He had something to look at, now. He checked on the HKBHSA projects. They were much into mining any number of things. Most were the kinds of things most people wouldn't consider when thinking of valuable minerals or such.

He remembered a book by Dave where the motive for murder was simply bauxite clay in a huge deposit. While gold was found in a nearby area that was the true motive, the figure for a small bauxite lode at only $3.00 per cubic yard seemed like next to nothing, but there were something like 14 million cubic yards of easy-to-mine bauxite. 3 X 14G, with the profit being $1.04 per yard. Forty two million bucks in two years was a hell of a motive for a relatively small Japanese company to knock off a couple of farmers to get their land (though that wasn't what happened in the book. It was one of the things considered by CD Grimes).

Bauxite wasn't as needed as a few years before, but that was an example that sprung to mind. Phosphorus was.

Phosphorus was mined in Georgia. The tumult in that area made doing business very difficult.

It was near enough to dinner time that Clint decided to have a good meal. Where would be a good place?

The Europa was supposed to have a very good restaurant. That seemed a logical choice.

There weren't many in the restaurant so early, so Clint walked around the nearby area a bit, then returned just before eight. The restaurant was doing a fairly good business, but there were tables available. One was almost next to a table where four men were just being seated. One of them was a fat bullish man who seemed to find fault with everything the girl seating them did. The other three didn't seem to notice. One had longish, very black hair and a tattoo of a tiger on his arm. He had on a "muscle" shirt to show the shoulder joint. He had several gold chains and fancy rings and a gaudy watch. The watch was a knock-off Rolex. There were a lot of them in Panamá.

The other two were the "yes men" type, to look at them.

Clint sat at the smaller table nearby, with his back toward them. He moved the bright chrome napkin holder to where he could see them in the reflection. It was to one side, and he wouldn't be seen looking at it. He had exceptionally good peripheral vision that had stood him in good stead many times before.

The restaurant was fairly quiet. He could hear a little, now and then, particularly when the fat pig was giving an order or ranting about the terrible service in this backward savage place, mostly in English. He did say things in three other languages, now and then. French, and what Clint assumed was Russian. Clint didn't remember Georgia as being world-sophisticated in any way. Or particularly modern, as to accommodations.

Of course, he wasn't among the elite the few days he was there thirty years ago. He didn't get to go to the classy joints, assuming there were any.

Victor soon called the dark-haired one "Blackie" – which Clint expected the minute he saw him. The blondish larger yes-man was Allen. The nerdy (did anyone say that anymore?) one was Dennis. They called Victor "Sir!" Strictly.

Victor took out a big Cuban cigar as they were waiting for desert, and was lighting it. The girl was signaling to the doorman, and Genio and a police officer were just coming in the door. Clint winked at Genio. The doorman said something to the cops. Clint heard the part, "... refuses to do it!"

Genio went to the table and slapped the cigar out of Victor's mouth, which drew gasps from several nearby. Blackie jumped up, and was reaching into his back pocket. Clint remembered that the Indios had taken a gun away from him. Now the officer with Genio did the same, but he didn't just grab it away, he twisted Blackie's arm up until Clint was sure he'd break it or tear it out of the socket. Blackie dropped the pistol and screamed.

"You, sir, and your thug, are under arrest. If these two wish to comment, I can include them!" Genio said in Spanish. Victor cried that he didn't speak Spanish (not true! Clint heard him speak it very well, if strangely accented) so Genio repeated it in his precise English.

"Who in hell do you think you are!?" Victor demanded. "I'm going to have you locked up in your own cell!"

"I think I am a representative of the Policia Nacional, that you are breaking the law that is very clearly stated in signs all over this and any restaurant here (pointing to the "Fumando prohibido" sign six feet away, on a column). I think your thug may not have a weapon in this country, and that he has attempted to threaten myself and this officer with one he was carrying concealed on his person – which is good for four years in the penitentiary. You will only have to pay a five hundred dollar fine and serve ten days, to this point. Should you wish to further expand the charges, you may do so now."

A rather smooth-looking tall, thin, dark man came into the restaurant then, and came over to say, "Capitan Genero, I believe? I spoke to you about my aeroplane being shot. What seems to be the problem here?"

"I came here merely to ask you a question or two about your lies concerning your purpose here. Martin, the doorman, was coming in to tell this vacuous pig he may not smoke in the restaurant. I removed the cigar from his mouth, this thug threatened myself and my officer with a pistol. I have placed them under arrest. They will be charged, and will serve their time. I still have the questions for you, Mr. Duquesne."

"Er, lies? About my purpose here? I don't...?"

"You are flying an avion that was much like one reported as having shot and killed two Panamanian citizens in the comarca. You stated you are a tourist with no interest here, yet you fly an avion carrying the same logo as another that was shot down by the Indios when it attacked them. You told me, personally, that you leased the avion to yourself as a tax dodge in Argentina. I have checked with Argentina. They say there is no advantage of any type for such a thing. The taxes and fees are the same for business and for private avions.

"I wish to learn what you were doing flying so very low over the comarca.

"Any further attempts to deceive me will result in charges. Is that clear?"

Clint smirked slightly for Genio to see, stated he certainly didn't think the restaurant in the Europa was a thuggy criminal hangout, Goodbye! and walked out. He was dying of curiosity as to what Genio was doing, and if it was somehow to his advantage. He'd learned a bit about Duquesne! He knew what that was about! It was definitely for his own edification. Genio had made it a point to act like he didn't know who Clint was.

Did the bit with Victor and Company just happen? He didn't see how that could have been set up.

He stood near the entrance until Victor and Blackie were shoved into the police truck, Victor yelling that he would take very strong action against all of Panamá for this insulting and demeaning attack on a poor private business-man here simply on vacation!

"Then you can explain about your going to the comarca and threatening the Panamanians there and saying you were going there with equipment whether they liked it or not, because you are so important and powerful. They removed another weapon from your thug and chased you from their land with bamboo canes? That should be interesting.

"I never act from personal suspicions. I must have cor-roborative facts.

"Now. Threaten me again and I will add that charge, and you will spend a year in penitentiary. Though it is not required here, I advise that you do or say nothing more that will be used in evidence against you in court."

Victor looked shocked as the truck drove off. Duquesne, Allen, and Dennis were standing in the entrance, staring in disbelief. Genio turned to them when the truck was gone and said, "Mr. Duquesne, I still require answers from you.

I will give you some time to think up a story that is not so laughable, or to tell me the truth. You may, meanwhile, not leave the bounds of Panamá City."

Duquesne and friends went back inside. Genio grinned at Clint and tossed his head toward the corner. He walked that direction and around the corner. Clint waited for a minute, then followed. Genio was talking with a man, and didn't look at Clint, so Clint passed and went toward the Hotel California. Genio soon came to catch up to him and say, "Meet me at the station!" as he passed.

Clint went on to the hotel, waited a few minutes in his room, then went down and into the restaurant door from the lobby and directly out the front when the view was cut off by the closing lobby door. He went around the corner and waited, but no one followed for a minute or two, then a man who had been lazing around the lobby came to look down the empty street. Clint was behind a large croton, out of sight. The man went back, and Clint went to the next corner and flagged a taxi. He went to the police station, where Genio was waiting in his office.

"Have you discovered what all this crap is about yet?" Genio demanded, as soon as Clint came in. "The damned Russian mafia seems to be involved!"

"I'm not sure, but I have a clue or two. They've found something on the comarca. That's obvious. I think it's probably phosphorus. Phosphate in huge supply."

Genio was silent, then went to his computer to study. He soon shrugged, and looked a question at Clint.

"Dave wrote a book where the motive for murder was a bauxite lode. It only brings three dollars a cubic yard, but there were fourteen million cubic yards on some farmers' property, or something.

"Phosphate is a little more, and the supply that's running out in Florida was billions of cubic yards. If there's a large lode, it will be in demand, and is easy to mine, though it's strictly a strip mine deal that makes a mess out of the environment."

"The Indios will, of course – and I blame them not – refuse allowance of strip mining on the comarcas. I foresee enormous problems. If they have a weapon such as you suggest ... I fear this greatly.

"I have to go to the comarca again. I want to see if that's what's going on. If it is ... I don't know what to do about it. The government's gonna get into it, and there will be horrible consequences for the Indios."

"Which is my dilemma," Clint agreed. "That weapon could mean that, for once in history, the little guy, the Indios, can bring the government to its knees!"

"The old story. If the natives had guns before the Spanish. It would be a very different world now. I begin to take seriously the Mayan calendar that ends civilization as we know it in December of next year."

"The timing seems about right – to a terrifying degree. I just wonder if it would be a bad thing for what we call civilization, that gives us Victor and drug deals and war, to end."

"It would depend on what takes its place."

Clint nodded slowly. He would go back to the comarca in the morning. He had to know a little more about the weapon, and about what those people had found.

"I wanted to ask if you set that bit with Victor and thuggy friends up in some way, or if it just happened."

"It was a rather fortunate coincidence. I was coming to question Duquesne to determine if he was connected. That isn't necessary, now. He would not have come to the table if he were not part of what they are doing."

"You can still ask him some embarrassing questions."

"I will keep delaying. He will then worry that I already know far more than he has considered. Perhaps he will find it hard to sleep if he is worried, which makes a person prone to making mistakes."

Clint nodded and grinned, made arrangements for the chopper at six in the morning, and left.

He considered, on his way back to the hotel in a dirty cab, what would be lost and what would be gained if civilization were actually to cease as we know it now. He was in a large modern city, very progressive, in one of the safest places on Earth – yet he wouldn't think of going on the streets alone in many sections at night. Contrast that to David, which was the second largest city. There was little (relatively) crime. It was safe to be most places anytime, though there was plenty of petty crime and schemes. Contrast them both to the comarcas.

No contest! The comarcas!

This had to be resolved, or at least understood. It was a long way into the fantastic science fiction scenario. So was television and computers and space travel a short time ago.

It was drizzling as they came into the village in the chopper. Roso came out to greet them and to tell Clint that he knew pretty closely where the company was concentrating. It was very flat land that was under a very shallow sea flat that was not in the water when the tide was low until the time of his great-great-great grandfather, when there was a great tremblor and the land rose. It was maybe three meters above the sea, now.

"It is in the coast?" Clint asked.

"No. There was sea, very shallow, for many kilometers in small bays and runnels that are no longer in the sea, though some near the shore of the sea are now going back into the sea. They were dry for many many years, but there is perhaps two centimeters of water there when the tide is high now."

"It is far?"

"No. Just past the lomas there (pointing to the southeast hills) maybe two kilometers."

"It's flat land now? Why couldn't they try to bring in their heavy equipment there instead of bothering the people who would stop them?" the chopper pilot, Ernesto, asked.

"Because it has much swamp on the whole place."

"How big is the flat land?" Clint asked.

"You will see. It is perhaps four kilometers across and three wide."

Ernesto said he would fly Clint over the area. Roso said that would be dangerous, because the chopper was to come to the village only, and would be shot down if it went farther. Clint told Ernesto they could damned well shoot him down. They could shoot down a stealth bomber, if what he suspected was true.

Ernesto would go back to Panamá City where he would tell Genio that phosphate was more than eighty percent likely to be the root of the problem. He would have to make a sounding probe to see how deep the deposit was.

Roso and Clint went to have a talk with the chiefs, later, then Roso would take him to the area. They were walking along the trail toward the spot when a small plane came in low. Roso pulled him under the trees as a Panamanian jet came to dive very close to the light plane. Roso made a call that was answered several places, and they waited. The jet circled and escorted the light plane back toward the northwest.

"I imagine Genio has given orders that any planes that come over the comarca at less than three kilometers are to be escorted back away, or shot down, if they refuse to leave."

"I think Genio is a good man," was all that Roso would say. They continued on through the little pass, and were on a large swampy flat area with swamp vegetation covering it. Roso made a call, and was answered. Three minutes later, two men and a young teenage boy stepped onto the path ahead of them. They spoke in the local dialect that Clint understood only a few words of, then Roso said there was a hole about three hundred meters into the swamp from the path. It was mucky and soft, but Clint had on finca boots, so they proceeded.

The hole was a slight depression with a 6" pipe sticking up a few inches in the middle.

"They did sonic readings," Clint said. "There will be

another hole like this close."

"There are four, this, and three more," Pedro, one of the men, said. Beto, the teenage boy, said, "One is by the hill there, and the other two are by the hills there (pointing across the swamp)."

"A complete sounding. They know within a few thousand cubic meters exactly what's here."

Roso nodded. "We can use the same places?"

"To make a sonic map? Oh, yeah! I'll have to call Genio to have sounding equipment brought in. Can you let the chopper land by the holes to set it up?"

"I will be done, but only that chopper," Roso agreed, then spoke to the others. The boy would stay to show them where the holes were. The two men melted into the shrubs.

"It will wait until no earlier than an hour past noon," Roso said, and they headed back toward the village. Clint climbed the nearest hill, but there was no signal. He went to the higher point past the village and called Genio to make the arrangements. Then Clint visited with his friends until the chopper came, about three thirty. He, Beto, and Roso joined Ernesto and Genio for a crowded flight to the holes. They set the recorders up, and Clint dropped the charge into the pipes while Genio and Ernesto took radiation background readings. They took the readings at all four places, then headed back. Beto stayed at the swamp, where Pedro came to watch the sounding. They dropped Roso off at the village and headed back to Panamá City.

"I have studied about phosphates," Genio said. "I found a great amount of information on the web. I now know that the supplies of the material is rapidly growing sparse. It would still seem a difficult and expensive thing that would return little. Six dollars and change per cubic meter. They would possibly construct a large processing plant on the area that would contaminate everything from there to the sea and much of the nearer Caribbean. There must be more to this than that."

"It's a matter of the overall amount. If it was only a meter deep, there would be about one hundred twenty thousand cubic meters. Not worth the expense. The figure they're working on is one that takes the average depth of the deposit into consideration. If it's ten meters deep, you're talking a hundred thousand two hundred times ten. That's a million and a quarter cubic meters. Borderline. If it's twelve meters deep, it's profitable. I suspect it's probably a lot more than that or they wouldn't be taking the chances they are. The Florida deposits are more than twenty meters deep, and are under twenty square miles. They've mined for nearly a hundred years. Billions of dollars."

Genio looked thoughtful, then nodded. "I don't know how to read the sonic map, but there were some long lines."

"I think we'll find the average depth is more than thirty meters."

"More than forty million dollars."

"That's for raw ore. If they process it, they'll get about a ton of triple super per two and a quarter cubic meters, which will sell at, the recent price, nearly a hundred bucks per ton. They'll add their transportation fees and clear about – clear, not margin – forty five dollars per cubic meter. They'll also produce phosphoric acid and such things that bring in another six or eight dollars per meter.

"Consider the way the price will increase when they close the rest of the Florida mines. We're talking a couple of billion dollars. Minimum."

Genio nodded. Ernesto said that seemed the kind of things those people would be after. They all agreed with that!

"It's an average of thirty two and eight tenths meters deep, give or take the eight tenths," Clint declared, after printing out and studying the sonic maps. I'd say three billion dollars over fifteen years at present prices. The price'll double in that time, so we're talking a *lot* of money.

"Yes. I'd have to work fifty years and would have that much if I were to be very frugal and inherit twenty five billion," Genio answered. "How will we deal with this stinking mess? They will undoubtedly try to bribe every corrupt politician and judge in the country."

"That means every politician and lawyer and most of the judges would get their part. Spread the money around.," Ernesto said, with a big grin. "I wonder how much they'll pay me not to see what they're doing when I fly over?"

"Maybe twenty bucks per trip."

"No way! I'll get fifty or I'll manage to see every move they make. I'm duty-bound to report it!"

"Make it sixty. I get ten – and I'll make your regular route four times per day over that very area!" Genio replied.

"Make it a hundred. You'll need that for me not to report this little conversation," Clint added. "Seriously, we have to make some kind of plan. I don't give a damn if the Indios shoot down everything that flies over the comarca, but I don't want ... I have to take a couple of days to run something down. The money may be the thing that's most important to them and to that type, but there's something else about this that has me worried."

"Yeah! What the hell kind of weapon do the indigenos have, and where did they get it?"

"I think I know part of the answer to that. I just hope I'm dead wrong," Clint said.

They talked about several plans, but didn't have enough information. The best and safest thing to do at the moment was see that no one went onto the comarca.

"I think I'll let Victor out of jail. I can say I hope he learned a lesson and blah, blah, blah," Genio suggested. "I think I want to know who he contacts. That could be very telling."

Clint nodded this time.

After a little more, Clint said he had to catch a plane to Bocas or David. He'd know which in a few minutes.

His cellular buzzed. He said that might be his answer.

It wasn't. Roso was calling to say four men came in a three-quarter ton truck to the almacen and were threatening people with guns. He said they would be buried by dark unless Clint wanted to know who they were or something. Genio and Ernesto were staring at the phone, that Clint had put on speaker, in disbelief.

"Keep all their stuff there. I'll come out in a day or two, so maybe we can find something about them. I suppose they'll be people someone hired to harass you."

"The truck is from Colón, and the driver and one other had cedulas issued in Colón."

"Blacks?"

"Yes."

"It figures!"

Genio said the situation was such that Ernesto would take him anywhere he had to go in the chopper. The Policia Nacional were requesting his help, and would pay for such things. This kind of crazy thing had to be stopped before it got completely out of hand. Clint said Bocas, first, to take care of unfinished business and see to his property and the projects in the area, then probably to David or somewhere.

They flew to Bocas, where Clint said they'd spend the night there, then go wherever they had to go in the morning. Ernesto could stay at Clint's place. Ernesto had a girlfriend in Bocas. He'd been stationed there twice before, once every two years on rotation. That would work out well for both of them!

Clint took care of his business, then took Judi Lum, his attractive nextdoor neighbor/helper with the projects and in his cases and all-around information gatherer extraordinaire out for a night on the town. They went to several places they frequented when there, such as Gringos, which was Gary's Mexican food restaurant, and the Toro Loco, Rip Tide, Refugio's, and the Lemon Grass. This case had nothing to do with the area, and no one knew anything, except that the Indios were shooting down planes that flew over the eastern comarca – so don't fly over the eastern comarca.

"I suppose that's an exaggeration. The Indios don't have anything that'll shoot down a plane!" Judi said.

"*Don't* be so damned sure. I think Dave gave them something. They *are* shooting down certain planes with certain company logos painted on the tail. They have damned good reason."

"You mean to tell me Dave's super weapon isn't just a story?"

"I hope to unholy hell it is, but don't think so. It's real. They *are* shooting down planes."

"Why do you think it's his idea?"

"Shooting them down is their own idea. He just gave them the ... whatever it is.

"Where is he? Do you know?"

"Cusapin. At least, I think so. He said he was going there, then to the coast east.

"Why do you think it was his super weapon? I suppose he's been in that area, but what would he give them something like that for?"

"He gave them that old Essex guitar, they have a serious problem the government's *not* going to help them with unless they're forced, they have something nobody can even figure that can shoot down planes, goes all the way through everything, and doesn't expand."

"Doesn't expand? Meaning?"

"It was either a very hard carbon steel or was traveling at a higher muzzle velocity than we can attain – or both."

"A child's marble wouldn't do it, then?"

"I asked about that point. It would have to be traveling at more than a hundred thousand miles per hour, but balsa wood would probably do it at that speed."

"It would take an atomic blast to get it that fast. An atomic blast would blow the gun up, and you could hear it for fifty miles. It would also kill the Indios using it."

"That's what scares me. It isn't atomic, and is something he says a ten year old kid could build with stuff you find around most houses. I thought it was one of his SF bullshit lines, but the Indios have something that's eerily like what he was talking about. I think he mentioned it in some of his SF books. I'm going to read a few of them. I remember something ... in two books. I've read eight or ten of those *Maita* books. It was used in a place where a court was being set up on an island ... I think I can find it. It'll give me a clue. Maybe."

"Maybe it's a good thing they have it. Dave's nuts, but not in a bad way. He wouldn't give them something they couldn't use with a lot of safety. He wouldn't, Clint."

"That's part of my dilemma. I know it. It's just that I don't want it in anyone else's hands. Ever."

"Another little piece. We're only a year and a half from the end of the Mayan calendar. I don't believe in most of that kind of thing, but too much is adding up to, as Dave says, zero."

"Well, they say it isn't the end of the world, just that it will go though drastic and unknowable change. That would do it."

"It would? How?"

"What if you didn't dare get on a plane, that no plane dared to fly? What happens to the world with only that?"

"And it could stop everything from a donkey to the stealth bomber, according to him. It could conceivably sink any ship. Any city could be starved out by a handful of nutcases – and there's one thing this world isn't short on. Nutcases! There'd be no way to deliver power that one person couldn't stop."

"I think most of that *is* SF. Enough of it isn't that it scares the piss out of me!"

"On the other hand, most of today's science fact was SF

a very few years ago."

"Shut the fuck up!"

She laughed and gave him the bird.

They went home a little after one. Clint got the CD with Dave's books on it and sat to look through the list and descriptions. It was that one. Book 39. It sounded like what the Indios had, so maybe it wasn't all SF. Maybe he had actually built the thing, like he said. In 1957. He then forgot about it until writing the books, and had used it in a couple. The problems he was having with his land being stolen and corrupt police and judges caused him to think seriously about building another one, just to see if 1957 was an accident or remembering something that didn't happen. He was toying with the idea of using the existence to force government to crack down on that corruption more than with a little lip service.

Apparently, it wasn't that! Crap!

Four thirty, so why bother going to bed. He'd get a new pot of coffee on, eat a good breakfast, then go through the day. He did that, at times. It didn't bother him to miss one or two nights sleep.

He called Ernesto at eight to say they were headed for Cusapín as soon as he could be ready. It seemed he was at the chopper to check it out, anyhow, so Clint threw a few things in a bag and headed to the airport. They were landing in Cusapín a few minutes after nine. Clint met with Basilio and Silvio, who was visiting there from Rambala, and found that Dave was somewhere to the east, no closer than fifty five kilometers, because that's where he left off last time. They took Nando's boat, so it would be easy to find them from the air. The boat would be on the beach, and they had those blue tents.

Twenty five minutes later they spotted the three tents and boat, so landed on the beach, a few hundred meters away. Dave was running a small gas generator to recharge his camera and laptop batteries while he worked on downloading the pictures and putting tags on the photos. He greeted them and said he'd be through in about half an hour. Coffee in the pot.

Nobody, and that was *nobody*, distracted Dave when he was working. He'd go ballistic!

They chatted with the two Indio boys helping Dave until he was through with the comp and had put the recharged batteries back in the camera and put the used ones on the charger. He asked Clint what he wanted that was so important he flew all the hell the way out there.

"Do you think it was a smart idea to give the Indios that electronic sling?" Clint asked.

"They won't let it out of their hands, and they won't try to figure how it works. I made a few things in it that means they'll mess it up if they try to get inside.

"They're using it?"

"Twice ... three times."

"Over the strip mine?"

"Over *a* strip mine. One that a bunch of greedbags want to open near Green Water. Phosphate."

"Hmm. Yeah. I kind of wondered about that area. It's a lot like Riverview was in the late forties and into the early fifties. I was born in Lakeland, and we used to swim and fish in the pits. We did for years. It wasn't until the seventies that we found out we were all supposed to have died from ten different cancers. There's radium in phosphate, you know.

"That area's a big wasteland that's supposed to be poisoned for the next few thousand years – so they're now putting some big developments on it.

"The sling's safe enough, for now. I suppose they'll eventually take it apart. It's obvious what it is, if they do."

"You only gave them one?"

"Uh-oh? They've already taken it apart?"

"Uh-huh. They have several."

"They'll keep the deal, Clint. It's still safe."

"Until someone else gets their hands on one. Welcome to the end of the Mayan calendar!"

"Could be! I'd recommend, pointedly, that you and our friends manage to come onto the comarcas, if that happens. It'll get pretty rough in the, you might say facetiously, civilized places."

"You aren't worried?"

"I didn't do anything. The damned thing's so obvious I'm totally amazed nobody thought of it a few hundred years ago! It's like trisecting the angle. They hadn't done it because it can't be done, so there! It took me all of fifteen minutes to figure that one. Big fucking deal. Anything anybody does with it's because they're what they are. It'll be people wanting revenge for some reason or other, ninety percent understandable and maybe justified by karma or something. It'll make this research pointless."

"So. You might as well give it up."

"No. I'll do it, because it's what I do. Screw the world and its problems. They're self-imposed. Prisoners of their own device, as The Eagles said."

Well, Clint had that answer. He was damned if he had a clue about what to do with it. They chatted awhile, then Dave and the kids went off into the rain forest and Clint and Ernesto headed for Panamá City.

"I'll go to the comarca and try to convince them that this is too big for anyone to handle. I won't have much luck, but they'll be a lot more careful. They know I wouldn't do anything to harm them in any way."

"If you're serious about this thing ... I think I'll want to make my friends in the comarcas or, at least, a long way from the cities. If we didn't have those holes with no expansion – I spent ten hours learning what that was about. The more I learned, the more scared I became – I'd say go fuck yourself. Tell it to someone stupid enough to believe the crap on the net.

"Clint, do you think it's possible to stop it? The Indios can be the most stubborn people in the world when they think they're in the right."

"That's the trouble here. There's no way I can believe they're *not* in the right. Can you picture what this world would be like if the Israelis or the Arabs or Afghans or whatever found the thing first, say fifty years ago?"

"Did they have the technology then?"

"According to Dave, we've had the technology since the early eighteen hundreds or decades before. According to him, there were probably thousands of ways this or that person tried to make one and it wouldn't work because of a basic law of the universe or something. He calls it reactionary repulse, and that it's the thing that makes electric motors work. I don't begin to understand it, but he says the only reason no one's ever been able to do it was because they looked at it from the wrong end."

"What the hell does that mean?"

"I don't have a clue. He says that it's all the same

equation where we decrease time by increasing velocity, and that's not efficient. Increasing velocity by decreasing time is efficient."

"Do you think they can make more without him?"

"He gave them one and warned them not to try to take it apart. He put something in it that would make it fail if the thing, whatever it is, was opened – but just looking at it would tell anyone with a brain what it was and how it worked."

"But ... they have several."

"Exactly."

"Shit! Fuck! Oh, Christ!"

"That pretty well covers it."

"I suppose all we can do is try. I also studied a little about phosphate mining. It can be pretty hard on an area."

"Yeah. That's precisely why I can't argue that they're wrong. They aren't. They're only trying to protect their land and themselves. They're only trying to keep the greedbags out. The trouble is, I can't think of any way phosphate can be mined that isn't your basic strip mine that'll leave pretty permanent destruction of a whole area."

"I'd bet they would be willing to dig the stuff by hand and wheelbarrow and leave the land ... but they'd take it away. They'd have to bring in fill or let it turn into a lake ... that would have to be diked to keep the contamination from killing the reefs for hundreds of miles. That would be a disaster of a magnitude that's almost impossible to imagine!"

"It would make Chernobyl look like a minor distraction," Clint agreed. "It would take a few years to begin to show the damage in a dramatic way, and then it would be far too late to stop it."

"If it were inland, where there was a good chance it could be contained permanently, I'd say we need the phosphate, so we have to make practical decisions, and all that bullshit. That isn't on that comarca. It isn't inland. It would be in the Caribbean the first hard rain, which only happens there two or three hundred days per year. It's a damned rain forest area!"

"But ... do you have any idea how much *money* we're talking about here?! Where the hell are your priorities?! Don't you know *money*'s the most important thing in life?! What turnip cart did you fall off of?"

That got him a bird with a twist!

They chatted awhile, then Ernesto said he'd get the chopper checked out and they could head out in about two hours. He'd drop Clint off on the comarca and return to Panamá City. He wasn't Clint Faraday and wouldn't be welcomed on the comarca, what with this crap. They had to agree about that.

Ernesto flew off. Roso looked at Clint in a speculative way, and asked what the problem was now.

"The sling. It's more dangerous than you know – not because of anything you would do or it would do, but because it could possibly destroy civilization as we know it if it gets in the hands of certain others – and it will, eventually."

He nodded knowingly. "It is my greatest concern with the thing. It is necessary, then will be removed when it has done what it must do."

"Which is put an idea into peoples' heads that it would be very much beyond stupid to mess with the comarcas." It was a statement. Roso nodded again.

"Clint, my good friend, we have made a solemn promise that one has broken, already. We promised our benefactor that no other would be made, but one has broken that promise. He has been disciplined. He will never again make one of the things, and will tell no one else about any part of it.

"It is a very surprisingly simple and relatively small device. It depends on one small thing to be correct and exact, or it will not work. The person who made the others feared he had destroyed our only hope when he took it apart because our benefactor had made something inside that moved things when it was opened. It was by luck alone that he was able to figure the correct positions. He said it made vibrations that must be in exact alignment. That was the importance of the parts being moved even a small bit.

"I do not know of such things. All I know is that it uses a battery to make objects move very fast in a straight line, so that we must never use it where it may make a hole in something many kilometers away. It must be up or down or with a very large mountain behind."

"It makes things move very fast. I don't know how."

"By inducing eddy currents is all I have heard – which makes little to no sense to me."

"It doesn't help me much, either," Clint replied. "How do you induce an eddy current in a non-conductor?"

Roso shrugged. "I understand nothing of what you said."

"But the person who took it apart was able to make it work? How?"

"By a mathematical thing that produces fractal logarhythms."

"Say what?!"

"My reaction exactly. Shall we have some hot fresh coffee and fishcake? I have to work in the fields now."

They went into the house, had the delicious snack, then Clint went with Roso to help make a new plot to plant several varieties of beans. He couldn't think of any way to get more information, but was eaten up by curiosity about how the sling worked. He had seen Dave pick up a marble the kids had been playing with in the street to say, "To think an object like this can shoot down a bomber or sink a ship is almost beyond belief – but it can."

That seemed to have been demonstrated.

How do you induce an eddy current in glass?

Of course, he didn't say "with this." He said "an object like this."

Still, the object was a glass marble.

It used a battery. What size?

It damned well sure wasn't any "AAA" size!

They had a charger, albeit a trickle charger. He'd used that to charge his laptop batteries and his cell phone. Did they have a bigger one?

He'd come up with the sling about the time he did the trisection of the angle. Did that math have a part of it?

Arc "A" plus Arc "C" divided by two equals arc "B" makes "B" the obvious trisection. It had been on the web and had gotten some attention by mathematicians, who said Pythagoras had shown it couldn't be done. They argued that it "seemed" to work, but couldn't overcome their education that said it couldn't. They finally decided he had only trisected the arc of the angle, not the angle – to which he replied, "How the hell do you trisect the arc *without* trisecing the angle?"

Dave said mathematicians had "proven" that a bumble

bee can't fly, and that a duck can't take off from the water. The bumble bee's wings are too small and the duck's wings are too far back on the fuselage.

For god's sake! Don't tell the bee or duck!

What a mood! He simply didn't know where to go from here. He concentrated on clearing the plot. It would wait until morning.

"Roso, I don't suppose you'd let me look at the sling?"

"You have. They had one while we were in the field yesterday."

"They didn't have anything but regular machetes and picks. And strainers. Let's see, the water barrel?"

"Roso, I saw it and didn't know what it was?"

"It looks like something you see everywhere. It can be made with things you find around many homes and shops. It is very simple."

"And uses a battery to work."

"Yes."

"What size battery?"

"It doesn't matter, but a smaller one will only work for one or two times. A larger one will work more, and will give more power. We use a car battery for most of them."

"Twelve volts?"

"It doesn't matter. Marine batteries are twenty four, and they work best, but are heavy."

"Crap!"

"What?"

"It's made of junk you find around the house and uses a battery that's handy anywhere in the whole damned world!"

"Clint, my dear friend, aren't you wasting time concentrating on the thing instead of the reason such a thing is necessary?"

That was a shock! He *was*!

"You're right. We have to find a way to keep that mine from ever happening."

"Which is why the device."

Clint nodded. He said he was going to the area of the phosphate to try to think of something, and went off in that direction. Emilio, a nine year old boy, said he'd go with him. They walked along the trail, talking about whatever came up. He'd seen the sling, and thought maybe he could make one, but he didn't know about some of the things inside. He wasn't really interested in that kind of thing. It didn't have any use, except to protect you, and there was only the need of that in the cities, except they needed it here.

"I'm going to try to take that need away. I just don't know how," Clint said.

"They will have to bring heavy machines here to dig it?"

"Yes. Certainly. Very large machines."

"When the time of the very high tides is here, the machines could not go there. They would sink."

"They could probably shore a part of it up for those times."

"Could you make the land stay wet and soft all the time?"

Clint looked at the little stream that ran across the swamp, and grinned. "Maybe! Just maybe!"

He spent four hours going all around the area. What he had in mind might actually work!

He checked the place where the stream went out between two mountains.

"I think we're going to have to come to a compromise

about the area, but maybe it won't be so bad," he said, on the way walking back to the village. "It depends on what's on those mountains where the stream goes through."

"Nothing. It is too steep to farm. Even cattle can't go there."

"That's almost too much to hope for. They can take anything we do out, but it would take a lot of time, and they would have to go all over the area behind the mountains, and even here. If they believe you have the sling, they won't. I can promise them worldwide publicity for what they plan now, and it would be too much if they had to expand it."

They went on into the puebla to find two police/soldiers and a foreigner arguing with Roso and an assortment of Indios.

"What's the problem here?" Clint asked. "Why are police on the comarca?"

"My questions," Roso answered.

"You're this Clint Faraday character?" the white asked.

"Uh-huh. And you?"

"You don't know what kind of trouble you're in for, shithead! We have government permission to come here, and we're coming here!"

Clint grabbed him by the shirt collar and yanked him up. "You threaten me once more and I'll legally tear your wimpy fucking head off. You and these clowns have no status here. You're illegal, and under comarca law. If Roso and my people think the lot of you should be executed for threatening us, you'll be executed. *They* are the law here! Got it?" He shoved him down to his knees.

"Shoot him!" the man screamed. "He attacked me! Shoot him!"

Clint kneed him in the mouth. He felt at least one tooth break. "They even act like they might someday maybe think about shooting anyone here and they'll be fertilizer in seconds. Get it through whatever passes for your brain that they're nothing on the comarca, and you're less!"

He turned to Roso. "What's this idiot's name? He tell you?"

Roso looked at some papers and said, "Sidney Portis.

"You think we should execute him?"

Portis was moaning and holding his mouth. He screeched again. It was dawning on him that the police weren't going to do anything. They had probably agreed to come along solely because Portis thought it would give him some kind of lever.

"That's always so messy, what with relatives coming to get the body and officials making us file reports and all that. He can go. This time. If he ever comes back onto the comarca, he will be executed. He has threatened us."

Clint winked at Roso where the police or Portis couldn't see. Roso turned and walked away. The other Indios followed him. Clint told the police officers to get Portis off the comarca and not to be so stupid as to bring anymore of the type there. One of the officers, who showed some Indio characteristics, hid a grin and said he wasn't about to argue the point. They didn't have any authorization, this time. Portis had hired them just outside the entrance road.

The other cop couldn't decide what to do. Clint walked off after Roso and the group and left them helping Portis to his feet.

Clint said he had a plan, but didn't know if it was feasible. They would talk about it tonight, and he would go to Panamá City in the morning.

They watched the trio leave, walking to the Land Rover not far from the village and heading out. Portis evidently wasn't going to drive the police back out with him, but one said something and unsnapped his holster. Portis got the idea. They drove off.

The rest of the afternoon was spent working in the field. When they got back to the village, the mood was grim. It seemed Pancho Salvez had been attacked and killed in Panamá City. They got the call just twenty minutes ago.

"That uncorks that fucking bottle!" Clint hissed. "Who?"

"They say it was a mugger, they believe."

"A mugger attacks an Indio? Since when? Indios don't carry money, and don't have jewelry or gold!" Silvio exclaimed.

"I seem to have another reason to go to Panamá City," Clint replied. He called Genio, who said he would check into it. It happened outside his district in a poorer part of the city. Clint said to send Ernesto after him in the morning. He had to get some things that would put an end to something that had gone much too far already.

"I'll need a few pounds of dynamite. I know I can't get plastics here."

"We can," Ernesto replied. "How much? What type?"

"I want to move some rocks. The whole sides of two mountains, really. C-four or better."

Ernesto called Genio, who said it would be supplied, but Clint would have to sign for it and ... what was it for?

"To stop a stupid war before it starts. A war between the indigenos and the government and some greedy companies," Clint answered.

"Well, that should be sufficient reason," Genio replied

drily.

They waited until an officer came, carrying a case. He said he was the explosives expert for the policia, so would do whatever Clint ordered, but they would not, could not, put that kind of high powered explosive into the hands of someone not registered as an expert in Panamá.

"It's not really in Panamá, it's in the comarca – but I don't know enough about it to do a decent job, so thanks," Clint said. "I'll want to drop the sides of a couple of mountains to make a ridge between them."

"For what purpose?"

"Let's tag it as establishing a fast and efficient road between two parts of the ... no. An access road to a large potential mineral acquisition area."

"I'm Oscar Menendez. Oscar. I like the way you think. For the Indios, it would be a big stink. For mineral access, it is a necessary operation.

"I thought you were all for stopping that travesty?"

"Well, they need a way to get in there. I just forgot that making the ridge would make the minerals unminable, because it would make it as much as impossible to use heavy machinery in the whole area. Bummer!"

"They won't just move the blockage?"

"Too expensive. It's fairly cheap to make the blockage, but would cost two-thirds of the profits to move it. Particularly when the Indios would make another five hundred meters away. "

He got a high five for that! They got in the chopper and went to the comarca. Roso had them wait an hour for the sentries to be informed, then they could do what they wanted. Roso mentioned that making the ridge road Clint planned would actually open a nice little chunk of arable land at altitude where they could grow some things they didn't have now. He went with them to plant the charges.

Oscar studied the area for three hours, carefully checking the kind of material and how to direct the charges for the best results. He said it was a type of operation not a lot unlike dropping a large building in downtown Panamá City.

It was 5:12 when he set the timers to blow two series of charges at one-half second intervals. One series on each side of the pass. The results looked like a natural ridge/bridge between two high mountains. One small section on the extreme end dropped a bit more than the sides. Oscar said there was a cave that collapsed and filled. They went to see in the chopper.

There were a lot of white rocks with wide grey streaks. Clint picked up a small one and said, "Shit! It's zinc! All we did was find another mine site.

"Well, this one won't cause much damage."

"This one won't cause any damage," Roso said. "It does not exist. We did not find any such thing here."

"I agree, except a survey plane will note this before the month is out," Oscar said.

"How will they see it?" Clint asked.

"Fly over. Depression with a lot of white rocks. No growth on them. No growth on the cover when it's on top like this. It's probably already noted by the satellites."

"No. There will be no such things!" Roso stated positively. "We must return to the puebla very quickly."

"What?" Clint asked on the way back.

"It is almost night. In the morning there will be only white limestone rocks and small brush growing in it. The same brush that is in all this area. It is only about a half hectare that must be covered. It will be done."

As soon as they landed, Roso called that all in the village were to come with him with any picks and shovels and buckets or wheelbarrows they had. It was to save the comarca. They would all work the whole night.

Clint didn't doubt they would do it. He said he had some urgent business in Panamá City. Pancho made it necessary for an explanation to be given. If retribution was due, it would be made.

"He was waiting for the bus at the terminal to go back to the comarca. He went around the end toward the bombas and didn't come back. His friend, Julio Hernandez, went looking for him and found him behind the trash containers there. He was stabbed four times," Genio reported. "We don't have anything to go on. The hoods who hang around there are known. All of them say no one would try to rob an Indio unless they saw him sell something for a lot of money or whatever. Salvez didn't have more than three balboas on him. Julio had the money.

"I sent an armed officer with him to the comarca, in case someone knew they sold about a hundred dollars worth of limes and yuca here. No one would bother him, that way. We just don't have anything, Clint."

Clint nodded and said he was going to check out a few things. Not as a police officer. Genio knew how that act worked. They wouldn't say anything they weren't forced to say to a cop, they would talk to a stranger. Maybe.

Clint grinned. "They'll talk to me. You don't know who to ask what."

Genio grinned and gave him the finger. "You're probably right."

Clint went to the terminal and walked around the end where Pancho was killed. He talked to a couple of people who were there a lot of the time, then went to the woman who directed traffic when it was heavy on that end of the terminal. He asked if she was working there the day and time Pancho Salvez was killed.

"Yes. I may have seen him go back there, but I'm not sure. A lot of people use it to urinate. You can tell that by the smell. They don't have a quarter to use the baños inside. We look the other way."

"I'm interested in anyone else who may have gone back there at the time. Anyone."

"Well, there was a man who came out. He may have come in from the other side. Well-dressed, or I wouldn't have paid any attention to him. He had a bandage on his face and a brace on his teeth, like when you have a broken jaw, you know? He was with Arno, I think."

"Arno?"

"A black man who sells lottery tickets – among other things."

"He around?"

"Probably around the entrance where the bar is."

"Thanks!" Clint waved and went to the far end of the terminal and asked the guard if Arno was around.

"I saw him over by KFC about half an hour ago."

Clint went inside and looked over the people hanging around the restaurants. Three or four could be Arno, so he asked a girl at the information booth who Arno was. She made a face and pointed to a tall skinny black with a lot of jewelry who was selling lotto tickets.

"Sort of a crud, huh?" Clint asked.

She grinned. "If you like understatement."

He went over to the man to come up behind him to say, "Getting involved with Portis is a good way to get dead. You know too much. That's what happened to Pancho Salvez. He knew too much."

He spun and stared at Clint, who was lounging against a column.

"You talk to me or you get shut up. Capiche?"

"Hey! He said the Indio was the one who broke his jaw!"

"*I'm* the one who broke his jaw. Watch your back. If you see him coming with someone like you, say whatever prayer you know, but it won't keep you out of hell.

"Caio!"

He walked off. Now to see what developed. Arno was going to feel he had to get the cops to help him or he was dead meat. That meant giving them Portis. C'est la vie!

"Clint? Genio here. I just wanted to tell you that the Portis character was found stabbed exactly like Salvez. Four times, any one of which is fatal. I suppose the Indios got even, huh?"

It was three days later, and Clint was back in Bocas Town. He had spent a day at the comarca, then Ernesto flew him home. He had four 3" PVC pipe sections about eight feet long with wires going inside. He didn't look inside. He didn't want to know. He gave them to Dave in Cusapín. It was on the way home. Dave said they did a better job than he did building them. He'd take them apart and use the PVC to deliver water to his plants.

They had flown over the zinc deposit area, which looked exactly like the surrounding territory. There were a few large white limestone rocks around.

"Arno still around?"

"Arno?"

"The one who killed Pancho, paid by Portis."

There was a pause. "I see. You set it up?"

"I tried to set it up where Arno would come to you to confess rather than be hit by a mysterious stranger hired by Portis. I guess he figured it would be easier and surer to get rid of Portis."

"You're something else!"

"So I'm told. I try to be practical."

"Hmm. Going fishing today?"

"I might."

C. D. Moulton's works are available on most major outlets as printed or e-books. CD writes the CD Grimes, PI mysteries, the Det. Lt. Nick Storie mysteries, the Clint Faraday mysteries, the Flight of the Maita science fiction series, books on orchid culture and many others of many types. Mystery, adventure, intrigue, science fiction, fantasy, paranormal, mild erotica, and factual.